NOT Hungry

KATE KARYUS QUINN

An imprint of Enslow Publishing

WEST 44 BOOKS™

Please visit our website, www.west44books.com.
For a free color catalog of all our high-quality books,
call toll free 1-800-542-2595 or fax 1-877-542-2596.

Cataloging-in-Publication Data

Names: Quinn, Kate Karyus.
Title: Not hungry / Kate Karyus Quinn.
Description: New York : West 44, 2020. | Series: West 44 YA verse
Identifiers: ISBN 9781538382691 (pbk.) | ISBN 9781538382707
  (library bound) | ISBN 9781538383353 (ebook)
Subjects: LCSH: Children's poetry, American. | Children's poetry, English. |
  English poetry.
Classification: LCC PS586.3 Q566 2020 | DDC 811'.60809282--dc23

First Edition

Published in 2020 by
Enslow Publishing LLC
101 West 23rd Street, Suite #240
New York, NY 10011

Editor: Caitie McAneney
Designer: Sam DeMartin

Printed in the United States of America

CPSIA compliance information: Batch #CS18W44: For further information contact
Enslow Publishing LLC, New York, New York at 1-800-542-2595.

FOR MY FOUR SISTERS.

I'M A LIAR

A liar who tells only one lie.

The same one
    again
        and
            again.

As I skip lunch
for the third time
that week.

Or pass on the tub of popcorn
—the biggest they offer—
as it travels between
    my sister,
            my mom,
                and I.

Or pick at
a piece of pizza
    before
        tossing it
            in the
                trash.

In all these situations
the same
        three
            words
                work.

I'm not hungry.

This is my lie.
A simple one.
A huge one.

Truth is:

I am
ALWAYS
hungry.

Truth is:

I'm starving.

I must be a good liar, though.

No one
  ever
    calls me
      on it.

MY BEST FRIEND LIKES TO GOSSIP

She's so anorexic.

Lacey whispers
as Stasia Keene
wafts by.

Caught shoplifting,

she says of
Dane and Darcy,
the Vinet twins.

She even knows the details.

Dane tried to get
        a power drill down his pants!
Darcy lifted her shirt
        as a distraction!

Usually, though,
it's less
reporting facts
and more
Lacey has a hunch.

Heard Simone Avet
        puking during
third period.
The upchuck diet is
        big with the Perfects.

Perfects.
That's Lacey's name
for the popular girls.

Bet she's trying to
*   size down*
*   in time*
*   for prom.*

Actually
we later learned
Simone Avet
was pregnant.

Lacey still claimed it
as a win.

I knew something was going on!

Lacey thinks
everyone
has secrets,
but really
she means everyone
who isn't us.

Never,
not once,
has she
ever
guessed
at mine.

When I have:
five baby carrots,
four bites of an apple,
three swallows of nonfat yogurt,
and one nibble
at the edge of an Oreo…

Lacey is
too busy
scanning the cafeteria
to notice.

Anyway,
what's there
to see?

Just another
fat girl
on a diet.

I NEVER LOSE WEIGHT

The best I can do
is misplace it.

Give it a month,
        maybe two.
I find it again.

Rounding out
        my hips
so my jeans
won't

    z

      i

        p.

Beneath my chin,
making mine a
D O U B L E W I D E.

Even at my
lowest,
I've never
been skinny.

I can't
stop trying
though.

My dream isn't to be
             a n o r e x i c.

But for people
like Lacey
to think I could be.

ONCE I DIDN'T EAT

for two whole days.

After my second night
not eating dinner
I passed out
walking up the stairs
to my room.

My mom was screaming.

Are you sick?
        We can't afford an ambulance!
                What's wrong?

So I confessed.

She went quiet.

Then finally she said,
softly,

Wish I had
    that sort of
        self-control.

Like she was…
                proud of me.

Once I won
the spelling bee
at school.

I brought a trophy home.
I was so happy.

But Mom
only glanced at it
and said,

Well, that's good
    I guess,
        but
            don't get
                too full of yourself.
    You're only spelling
        the words,
            not inventing them.

But the night I passed out
she helped me stand.
Put me on the couch.
Propped up
with a pillow.

Then she
heated
a can
of soup.

Chicken noodle
without the noodles.

She picked them out.

So I had
broth
and carrots
and a few
sad chunks
of gray celery.

*We don't want
all your hard work
to be wasted.*

She stroked my forehead
in a way meant to be motherly.

Except she wasn't that type of mother.

It just felt weird.

MY SISTER, MAE,

is beautiful.

She wakes up
two hours
before school starts.

Paints her lips
    dark red and ripe.

Her cheeks
    pink dots
        on glowing skin.

Long dark hair
    hangs down her back,
        in long, silky ringlets.

My sister, Mae,
    is beautiful.

Every day
    she wears
        a dress.

Polka dots
or
stripes.

Sweetheart neckline
and a nipped-in waist.

Wide flowing skirt
  and
    cute
      little
        kitten
          heels.

Like a glamorous
'50s housewife
on her way
to high school.

My sister, Mae,
    is beautiful.

Sometimes she'll
complete the
  perfect
     picture
with a plate
of brownies
she stayed
up late
to bake.

Not from a box, either.

It's her own
  extra
    gooey,
  extra
    chewy

triple
    chocolate
        brownie
            recipe.

Mae gives them
to her boyfriend,
Erick.

Er-
   ICK.

Emphasis on the *ick.*

Erick, star of the
wrestling team.
Neckless wonder.

A guy who says,
   Mae, get your
      fat butt
        over here.

Erick.

The love
   of Mae's
      life.

He gets Mae's
   specially
      baked
        brownies.

Erick eats
half
of them
while
handing out
the rest
like a king.

Everyone
at school
knows about
Mae's brownies.

Tweets go out:
        Brownies sighted!

Erick loves the attention.

And Mae loves him.

I guess
it all
works out
that way.

My sister, Mae,
        is beautiful.

She counts herself
        L-U-C-K-Y
to have Erick
in his varsity jacket.

Even when
he grabs her chest
in the middle of the
SENIOR HALLWAY.
And yells
HONK,
   HONK,
HONK.

My sister, Mae,
  is beautiful.

But she's a liar, too.

Because she
LAUGHS
and says,

It's
 just a
  joke.

OR

He
 doesn't
  mean it.

 OR

I don't
 mind,
  really
   I don't.

My sister, Mae,
        is beautiful.

And the
    BEST
        person
            I know.

Sometimes,
when my arms
are too heavy
and too tired
to lift up
and wash
my hair…

Mae will do it for me.

In the kitchen sink
like when
we were kids
playing
        beauty
            shop.

Her hands are
        soft
            and
                exact.

She combs out
the tangles,
then blows it dry, too.

My sister, Mae,
          is fat.

The doctor
actually said
she's obese.

Fat is ugly.
Everyone
knows that.

My sister, Mae,
          is a mystery.

She's both
     fat
       and
          beautiful.

She is completely herself.

Like she doesn't know
how else to be.

I once said to Lacey,

          Everyone
               knows Mae.
          And
          everyone
               likes Mae.
          So Mae must be popular.

Lacey laughed.

That's not popular.
            Popular is
    everyone
            wanting to
                    be you.

Our mom's sister,
our aunt,
who is both
        scary
            and
                skinny,
once told Mae
it was a shame
about her weight.
She could've been
        a real beauty.

Like Mae's beauty
was trapped

----under----
her own flesh.
And not sitting
        out
            on
                TOP
where everyone
could see.

I see it, though.

I see Mae.

And she is beautiful.

I ATE

The hunger was
        unleashed.

Usually it
        growls
and strains
at its
        chain.

Today it burst
        free.

I ate
all the leftover
takeout rice.

It fell out
of the container
solid like a brick.

I bit into it cold
as it crumbled
in my hands.

Scooping up the bits
that fell
to the floor,
I shoved them in, too.

It wasn't enough.

I ate
leftover
off-brand
Oreos
forgotten
at the back
of the cupboard.

I ate
the smashed
bits of chips
left at the bottom
of three
different bags.

I ate
instant pudding
mixed with milk
not waiting
for it to set.

And then
I licked the bowl.

I ate
bread.
Toasted
with butter
and honey.

Slice after slice.
Fast as the toaster
spit them out.

I ate
slices of pepperoni.
Old and crusty
at the edges
from that night
long ago
when Mae and I made pizzas
from scratch.

(Really Mae
made them
and ate them
while I watched.)

I ate
until mid-chew—

I
felt
IT.

Then I ran.

AT THE BACK OF OUR HOUSE

There's a row
of hedges
    HUGE
      and
        OVERGROWN.

I leave
a little shovel
out there
to quickly
re-dig
my hole.

"The purging place,"
I call it.

Where I bury my shame.

Now I throw up,
eating in reverse,
closing my eyes so
I don't have to see.

The ground is not like the toilet,
whisking all away
with a brisk flush.
It just takes it into itself.

Isn't that what dirt is anyway?
The guts of the earth.

The things underneath
we don't usually see.

SHAKY, I STAND,

wiping
   my mouth
      with the back
         of my sleeve.

That's when I see him.

A boy
near my age
lOOking
over
the fence.
STARING
at me.

His expression…
Unreadable.

I blink.
Once.
Twice.

Sorry, he says.
I heard…
I didn't…
I thought
   someone
      needed help.

I swallow.

My throat
   is raw
     and my mouth
       tastes
         like garbage.

I'm fine, I say.

My second lie.
A new one for me.

It's not convincing.

I give it another try.

Really,
       I'm
         fine.

A bob forward,
an awkward sort of bow.

And then I flee.

Back
into
my house
where I
BOLT
the doors
behind me.

It doesn't
　　help
　　　　to keep
　　　　　　my questions
　　　　　　　　　away.

Oh god.
Oh no.

Who the heck
　　was that?

And how much
　　did he see?

WORSE AND WORSE AND WORSE

He's at school
the next day.

I see him
in the hall
after first period.

Our eyes meet.
I look away,
my face burning.

At lunch
Lacey has
ALL the details.

Toby Watkins.
Sophomore.
Like us.

Popular.
UNlike us.

Basketball star
at his old school.

Lacey hesitates.

My breath catches.

This is it.

Toby told
EVERYone
what he saw
yesterday.

But Lacey
only sighs.

I've got bio
        with him...
he's
    really
        cute.

And I realize
she has
one of her
hopeless
  c
    r
      u
        s
          h
            e
              s
again.

On him.
Toby.
The new boy.

Who saw nothing.
Or maybe everything.
But said nothing
to anyone.

At
least
not
yet.

ONE WEEK PASSES

Then two.

Then three.

Toby
the new boy
becomes simply
Toby
the popular boy.
Someone with
no bearing
on my life.

Except
Lacey is
officially obsessed.

Lacey knows
Toby's
ENTIRE
class
schedule.
Lacey knows
his
middle
name.

She knows
he's allergic
to peanuts.

The next day
  and
    every
      one
        after,
Lacey packs
a cheese sandwich
instead of
her usual
PB&J.
Every time
she takes a bite,
I wonder
exactly what
she hopes
will happen
to make
this switch
worthwhile.

Lacey knows
he doesn't
have a
date to the
Homecoming
Dance
yet.

But he's going.

All the
student athletes
are encouraged
to attend
for
RAH RAH
GO TEAM
school spirit.

And Toby is
already part of
the basketball team.

Lacey explains
all this
breathless.
Eyes sparkling
behind her glasses.

We're joining the
    dance committee.

She announces this,
certain I'll say yes.

Only after
I shake my head
and make a face
does she add,

Please?
    Oh please.
I've got to be
    at this dance.

If we're on
    the committee
        we have an excuse
            to be there.

I sigh.

Or…
    we could just
        buy tickets,

I counter.

Lacey
shakes her head,
annoyed
I'm not getting it.

I don't want
    to just be there
            watching.
I want to be part of it.
I want to be
            seen.

I put down
the french fry
gone cold
after I've
fiddled with it
for 15 minutes
never taking
    a
        single
            bite.

In these last
three weeks
I've lost
12 pounds.

In these last
three weeks
I've watched
Toby, too.
Our eyes
keep snagging
as we
    C   C
     R   R
      I   O
       S S
         S S
the same
hallways.

He lOOks.
He sees.

It's getting
harder
and
harder
to look away.

I imagine
him
and
me
at the dance.

I imagine
our eyes
meeting
while
music pumps
and
lights flash.

I imagine
him saying…
          I don't know what.

But…
          I want to keep pretending
               I might find out.

I agree
to join
 the
     Homecoming
          Dance
               Committee.

I'M HOME ALONE

Mom's working
late.

Mae's out
with Erick.

This is when
I find it
hardest
to be
hungry.

This is when
I eat.

I pace
the kitchen,
  opening
      and
        shutting
          cupboard
            doors.

I want
to eat.

I want to
feel full.

But I can't.

I keep
looking
over
my
shoulder.

Certain someone
is there.

Certain someone
will see.

I cut
raisins
into
quarters
and chew
each
bite
20
times.

I drink
diet soda
and chomp
the
ice.

I pretend
it's enough.

THE DOORBELL RINGS

It's Toby.

TOBY.

Standing
on the cinder blocks
stacked outside
our front door.

Sorry,

he says.

I'm not—
I hope—
I don't—

He's upset.
Unable
to form
a full
sentence.

Finally,
he gives
himself
a shake.

My grandmother.

She fell
in the shower.

She can't
get up.

She won't
let me in.

There's
no one
else.

She said
to give her
a minute.

But it's
been thirty.

The words
fall out
 fast
   then
     slow
like he's
unsure
how much
to give
away.

All the while
I nod
stupidly.

Then
I realize.
It's my turn
to say
SOMETHING.

I panic.

I'm June.

Toby frowns.
Confused.

Hi.
I mean,
yeah,
I should've said
I'm Toby.
I live next door.
I figured you…

Knew.

He doesn't
say it aloud.

I hear it
anyway.

Of course
I know
who he is.

And he
knows me.

Maybe not
my name.
  But
    everything
              else.

Can you…
      help
        me?
        Maybe?

He breaks the
  a w k w a r d
              silence.

With your grandma?

He nods.

Yeah.

My face
is
flushed.

My palms
are
sweating.

Sure.
Yes.
Of course.
Happy to.
Yeah.
Let's go.

Lead
    the
        way.

It is
word
vomit.

How appropriate.

At least it works.

He turns.
I follow.

MY FRONT DOOR CLOSES BEHIND ME

We cross the grass
wet with rain.

His front door
opens
before me.

All the while
I wonder…

is this happening?

NAKED OLD LADIES

are slippery
and grumpy
and rude.

They yell
if you help
and yell
if you don't.

They snarl
and curse
and threaten
to bite.

They do
   NOT
      say
         thank
            you.

And yet
I'd help
a hundred
more
if every
time after
Toby
smiled
and said,

Oh wow,
   you saved
        my life.
Thank you.

Seriously,
   I owe you
        big time,
              June.

I shrug. Mumble,

No problem,

a million times
  and
     turn
        to
           leave.

Wait,

Toby calls.

You…
        busy now? Want to…
        hang out?

I nod.

Yes. Yes. Yes.

I do. I do. I do.

EVERYONE HAS SECRETS

Toby
talked
to me.

Everyone has secrets.

He said lots
before that,
but those
three words
stuck.

And left me
wishing
I'd asked,

What's yours?

THE NEXT DAY

at school
I see
Toby
in the hallway
between classes.

Our eyes meet
and hold.

Instead of
looking away,
I smile
and raise
my hand
to wave.

Suddenly,
Toby turns
back into
the empty
classroom
he just left.

My hand
    F
     A
      L
       L
      S
        to my side.

But the
stupid
smile stays
while I
keep walking
  down
      the
          hall.

Hanging
on my face
like a
light
  left on
      in an
          empty
              room.

THERE ARE TWO TOBYS

Lacey tells me
all about
Toby Number One.

Toby talked to me.
    Do you know
        what he said?

She sighs.
Then quotes,
"There's toilet paper
        on your shoe."
Wasn't that sweet of him
        to let me know?

I agree he's sweet.
But Lacey has already
moved on.

He's awful at math.
Maybe I should
        offer to
            tutor him?

He is awful at math.
I think this,
but don't say it aloud.

I know this because
Toby lies
on my bedroom floor
most afternoons
and groans until
I push aside
my own books
and help him
understand algebra.

This is Toby Number Two.

The boy who
leans in to me
and says,

Mmm,
  your hair smells nice.

The boy who
tells Mae
her brownies
are worth millions
and then begs
to lick
the spoon.

The boy who
makes me lick
that same spoon.
One for him.
One for me.
Passing it
back and forth
until finally

he says,

Last lick for you.

The boy who
breaks my heart
every day
when he goes
to school and...

Toby Number Two
reverts back to
Toby Number One.

The boy who
looks the other way
when we pass
in the hallway.

I'm not

falling for Toby.
I'm not that
much of an
         idiot.

Even as
we spend
more and more
time together.

I'm not
skinny.
But I am
      losing weight.
I'm not
hating it
when people notice
and say,

Wow, June, you look great!

Even Lacey notices.

You're not gonna
         eat that…
             right?

She points to the
ham sandwich
in my hand.

I've been poking
holes in the bread.
But haven't eaten
a single bite.

I'm not
going to say no
when Lacey's lunches
have been looking thin.

Sometimes toward
the end of the month
if her dad doesn't send
the child support check
she gets
half sandwiches
with just jelly
in between.

I push my sandwich
across the table.
Watch as she bites
into it.
    HUNGRY.

I swallow.

I'm not
    HUNGRY.
I'm not.

The cookies, too?

Lacey asks.

I pass them across
the table.

Her white teeth
bite into
the freshly baked
chocolate chip cookies.
They leave half-moons
around the perimeter
as she works
her way around,
nibbling away
until only the center remains.

Gracefully
brushing away
the crumbs,
she flicks a look my way.

You do look good, June.
But you can't just diet.
Eventually
*   you need*
*   to exercise, too.*

I'm not
the type
to tell Lacey
where to shove
her helpful advice.

I'm not
the type
to tell her
I've been

55

hanging out
with her
      secret
        crush.

But if I were.
Oh, if I were.
I can just imagine
    the
      look
        on her
          face.

BASKETBALL BEGINS

and Toby disappears.

No more after-school homework
while lying on
my bedroom floor.

No more
Wheel of Fortune
with his Grandma
beating us both
every time.

No more
distractions
from Erick
fighting
with Mae
in the next room.

(*Hey*, he says.
*You gave the brownies
to me.
I can sell 'em
if I want to.*)

(Mae answers,
*Of course,
They're yours. I just didn't understand.
Do you need money?*)

(*Mae, you dope,*
he says,
tenderly,
I suppose.
Everyone needs money.
A pause.
Then he adds,
casually cruel,
Anyway, I'm
sick of brownies.
Doncha know
how to make
anything else?)

No more
ability
to ignore
the
  pan
    of
      lasagna
forgotten
at the back of the fridge.

I eat it cold.
Scooping
handfuls,
sucking
red sauce
from my fingers.

For the first time
in a long time
I feel full.

It's wonderful.
And wrong.
Bad.

Then worse
as my stomach swells,
pushing against
the belt
I now use
to keep my pants up.

The lasagna comes back up
even
    faster
        than it
            went down.

Into the kitchen sink.
Down
    the grinding
        garbage disposal.

Afterward,
I stand looking into the
empty sink.
Feeling empty.
But not better.

I've just finished
washing the pan
when there's a
knock at the door.

It's Toby.
I know it.

Another knock.

I creep toward
Mom's room.
Her window looks
out toward the
front of the house.

    Carefully

      parting

    the blinds

      I

      peek

      out

There's Toby,
his head bent
over his phone.

We only
exchanged numbers
last week.

He put me in his phone
under the heading:
CUTE GIRL.

It was a compliment.
No boy had ever seen me
as anything other than fat.

It was also a lie.
He didn't want my name
in his phone.
He didn't want anyone
to see JUNE listed.
To know
he knows me.

My phone rings.

Quickly,
I silence it.

I wait
and watch as
Toby knocks
once more.

I wait
and watch as
Toby walks
away.

I'm
  devastated.
I'm
  relieved.

Mostly
I'm
  tired.

Tired of being
        HUNGRY.

And tired of wanting
        what I can't have.

A WEEH PASSES

I stay busy
with Lacey
and the Homecoming
Dance Committee.

It turns out
I'm good at
planning Homecoming dances.

I make a poster
using my laptop
to cut and paste
the heads
of football players
and cheerleaders
onto the bodies
of knights and ladies
to match our theme of
Ye Olde Homecoming.

Everyone is impressed.

I don't tell them
I learned this skill
while pasting
my head onto
skinny models.

Lacey helps.

She knows
everyone
and where to find
their pics online.

Oh, his Instagram is
            sooo good,

she says.

The committee members
tell us
we need to help with
ALL
the dances
from now on.

Lacey is thrilled.

Actually,
I am, too.

It makes
me realize:
Maybe
I've made
my life
smaller than
it needs to be.

Walking home
I'm thinking about
Homecoming throne
construction.

I've forgotten
completely
about Toby…

Until I get home
and he's in
the kitchen
with Mae
as she works on
the perfect
shortbread cookie,
explaining to Toby,

I can mix it up.
Add chocolate chips
or fruit
or nuts.
That way,
it's never the same.
That way,
Erick won't
get sick of it.

Toby,
seeing me,
winks,
then tells Mae,

I can't imagine
anyone
getting bored
with you.

Mae flushes.
Not me.
He's not bored
          with me.
We're good.
We're great.
It's the brownies.
You can't expect him
          to eat brownies
                    all the time.
I should've known.
So stupid of me.

Mae catches sight of me.
I must look mad.

What's wrong?

she asks.

Instantly concerned.
Worried for me.

I can't tell her
I want to
murder ErICK.
Or that I want
Toby gone.

Nothing,

I say.

I'll just miss the brownies,
I say.

Me too,

Toby adds.

Don't let Erick
ruin them
for the rest of us.

He stresses the
                    ick
            in Erick.
Just the way I always do.

I do not let my heart lift.
Even as Toby turns to me
                    and says,

I've been waiting for you.
Want to go for a walk?

I should make an excuse.

Homework.

It's too cold.

Or just a no
with no excuse
attached.
Just no.

Behind Toby's back,

Mae grins at me.

The
     June-has-
          a-boyfriend
grin.

I shake my head
at her.

Toby doesn't
like me
that way.

Even if he did…

Look at what Mae does
to hold onto Erick.
What would it cost me
to keep Toby?

C'mon,

Toby nudges me.

A quick walk,
     I promise.
You'll love it.
There's lots of
     crisp leaves
          to crunch.

I told him
weeks ago my favorite part
of fall
was walking on
fallen leaves
hearing them
crackle like Rice Krispies
beneath my feet.

He remembered.

Okay,
    I say at last.

Because sometimes
it's too hard
to say no.

Because sometimes
            it's too easy
                    to pretend
girls like me
    (and Mae)
        get happy endings,
        too.

WE WALK IN SILENCE

Listening to the leaves
crunch
with every step.

I shiver from the cold
and Toby plops his hat
onto my head.

It grows dark.
Toby takes my hand.

My empty stomach
                    aches.
My toes go numb
        inside my shoes.
But I don't suggest
        we turn back.

As long as
Toby
holds my hand
I'll walk
with him
wherever
he wants to go.

My heart sinks
when he stops.

There.

He points across the street.

It's just a house.
That's all I see.

Gripping my hand
harder,
he pulls me
across the street
until we're
in front of the house.

SUDDENLY, I GET IT

The lights are on.
The curtains are open.
We can easily see in.

The mother is vacuuming.
Two kids are on tablets.

A man enters.
He slaps the mom's butt.
When she whirls around,
he kisses her.

The kids don't even look up.

She pushes him away.
But he comes back,
taking the vacuum
from her,
tossing it aside.

Then grabbing her hands,
           he starts to dance.

She resists…
           until she doesn't.

Her arms   come around
     his neck.

They
sway
in the
middle
of the room.

The kids are still unaware.

But Toby and I watch it all.

It's like they're on a stage.

When they finish,
I clap.

OH, THAT WAS GREAT,

I say.
Do you know them?

Toby laughs.
Of course not.
That would be
creepy.
I only spy
    on strangers.
The stranger the better.

I wonder if he's
talking about me.

About lOOking
over the
hedges
and watching me
heave.

But then he takes
my hand again,
pulling me further
down the street.

Helpless,
I follow where
he leads.

WE WATCH

an old couple
as they sit
on their couch
at opposite ends.

They eat soup,
awkwardly
cradling the bowls
in their hands.

The TV flickers
with something
we can't see.
They stare at it,
unblinking.

We watch
so many people
watching their
televisions.

Game shows.
      Sitcom repeats
            from 10 years ago.
                    The nightly news.

We watch until
it's fully dark
and now almost
all curtains

and blinds
are closed.

I wait for Toby
to call it.
To say it's time
to head home.

Instead,
twitchy and tense,
he stomps his feet
and
mutters
      under his breath.

Hesitant,
I
   reach
         out,
touch his sleeve
  lightly.
Then
snatch
  my hand
back.

What's wrong?

I ask.

Sighing,
he runs a hand
through his hair.

Everyone is boring.
I wanted it—
I wanted you—

He stops.
Shrugs.

He's embarrassed,
I realize.

It's okay,
I say.

No.

He shakes his head.

I wanted you to get it.
I thought
you'd get it.
Cause you're…

I hold my breath,
desperate to hear
what I am.

Instead, he goes
off
in another direction.

I took a friend
        once
   back where I used
            to live.

She called me
                    a freak.
Said it was wrong.
Said I was sick.

I told her,

Hey, I'm not
        hurting anyone.
I'm just interested,
                    you know.
Like curious.
I want to see,
    to know
        how other people
                            live.

But more than that—

Toby paces now,
        punching his hands
                    fist to palm.

He barely
notices me,
shivering from the cold.

More than that
I go out,
    find the nicest,
        most perfect house
                    filled with
                        perfect people.

Mom and Dad.
Nice cars parked
straight and clean in the driveway.
Lawn cut even and trim.
They got two kids.
Little ones.
Boy and girl
in private school uniforms,
getting on the bus
waving to Mom and Dad.

Everyone happy-happy,
grinning big
and so perfect
it hurts to see it.

To think it might be true.

Toby's voice is
too loud
on the quiet street.
But I don't
shush him.
I listen
and let him rant.

So one night
I can't take it
at my house.
I go out walking.
It's late.
and everyone's
snug inside.

*Happy families
doing
happy family
things.*

*I go by the house
of the
perfect family
in their
perfect house
with their
perfect kids.*

*I pick up a rock
out of their own
landscaping.
It's heavy in my hand.
I go closer,
thinking to put it
through a window.*

*That's when I hear it.
Shouting.
From inside the house.
And a kid.
Crying.   Wailing.
Scared.*

*I creep closer
and now I see
they got filmy type
curtains
you can almost see
right through.*

There's a man
    shaking a lady,
        she's screaming,
        kid at her feet
is sobbing.
It's awful.

And it's also
            kinda perfect.

Toby laughs.

Misery loves company,
            isn't that what they say?

He laughs again,
but then it trails off
as he finally looks
                over
at me.

His eyes
    hold mine.
Intense.
Burning
    in the dark night.

I nod.

Yeah.
    That's what they say.

He comes closer,
   his hands
grabbing mine
   holding them
to pull me closer
   pulling me into
      him,
   then his hands
   are over my ears
shushing the world
      and I think
he's warming them
   but he wants me
      closer still
   'til our lips touch.

                        He kisses me.

I'm so shocked
   I stand there,
      stupid
   and unmoving.

Days
and years
and decades
pass
before some
voice
in my head
yells,

Kiss him back, stupid!
So I do.

The best I can.
All the while
 certain
  I'm doing it wrong.

Finally,
just as I'm
getting the hang of it
(I think I'm getting the hang of it)
Toby pulls back.

His hands caress my face
 and it's weird
  and wonderful.

His eyes   stare into
  mine.

You get it,
 don't you,
  June?

You see someone
 or something,
  they seem perfect
   but they're not.

Or like you.

His thumb
brushes my lips.
And I'm barely
listening to what
he's saying.

People see you,
    and they think
        they know you
            or about you.
Like you're lazy
    or
        addicted to fast food.

Suddenly Toby's flow
    of words
                    ….stalls…

I realize I've pushed him.
My hands against his chest.
Shoving him away from me.

That's what people think?
Or what you think?

The words come
from lips still warmed
with his kisses.

My voice is soft.
Only trembling
                slightly.

Toby swallows.

No it's other people.
They think…
It's not,
    I mean,
        you're not
            like your sister.

84

Like Mae.
Making brownies.

Like, of course,
the big girl
loves dessert
and makes the
best brownies.
But you…

He trails off again.
I wait.

But you…
you're not like Mae.

You try to be…
                different.
You don't eat
like she does.

I mean,
    you probably
                just have
                    bad genes.

I laugh.
I don't know why.
Because really,
I want to cry.

Bad genes,

I repeat.

Wondering
if he can hear it.

How incredibly
STUPID
it sounds.

But Toby nods
        eagerly
            like we're on
the same page.

Yeah, bad luck.
Right?

He says.

Worst luck,

I answer.

The very worst.

WRAPPING MY ARMS

around myself,
I turn
and
do
what I should've
done
long ago.

I walk away.

TOBY'S NOT THE TYPE

to go rushing after
a girl
calling her name
and babbling
apologies.

Toby's the type…

                    to wait.

Let you walk alone
several blocks,
before finally
catching up
and falling
into step
beside you.

Like nothing ever happened.

Like you imagined everything.

Toby is so good
            at pretending.

I'm a friend in one place.
A stranger in another.

I'm the girl
who gets him.

The girl
he kisses
in the dark.

The girl
who will—
of course
—easily
forgive him.

I STOP

Toby keeps walking
several paces,
not realizing
I'm no longer beside him.

I watch him
striding forward
loose-limbed and
confident.
He's so certain
I'm still
trotting along
beside him.

He actually
startles
when he finally
looks to his side
and realizes
I'm no longer there.

Ha.

Whipping around,
he throws his
arms out.
And I can tell
he's mad.

Mad at me
for making him
        look foolish.

C'mon, seriously? You're still pouting? You want some
        BIG APOLOGY?
Is that it?

No,

I respond.

I want you
to take me
to
 the
  Homecoming
        Dance.

Toby's arms fall.
He wasn't expecting that.

Honestly,
I wasn't either.

The words
fall from my mouth
before I can
stop them.

June…

Toby says.

Just that.
My name
            and nothing more.

I could
        let him
                off
        the hook.

Say I'm joking
or something.

But I don't.
Instead, I just wait.

OKAY, LOOK,

Toby says.

I don't wanna go
    to Homecoming
        at all.
But I gotta
    because of basketball.

So, I'm going
    with a group
        of friends.
Not people
    you really know.
Guys from the team
    and their girlfriends.
It'd be weird
    and awkward
        if I had you
            as a date.
When everyone
    is treating it
        more casual.
Like a thing
    your parents
        are making you do.

Toby   finishes
    with   a
        shrug.

Okay.

That's what I
should say.

Let it go.

Instead,
my mouth
decides
tonight is the night
I say what needs
to be said.

Why did you kiss me? Do you even like me?

The   words
    hang   between
            us.

Then Toby strides
                toward me
closing the distance.

*Do you think
    I kiss girls
        I don't like?
Do you think
    I hang out
        all the time
    with girls
        I don't like?*

I like you, June.
I like you
  so much.
I like you…
  more than I should.
If things were
  different…

My nose is
running
from the cold.
And from
the tears
filling my eyes.

Like if I were skinny,

I say.

Different like that,
     right?

Toby grabs my arms.
TIGHT.

No!
Not like that.

I shouldn't
  have said that before
   about
bad genes.

What I meant was…

You got secrets.
Ugly ones.
Ones that
make you
different.

That set you
                apart.

I got those kind of
secrets,
too.
Don't shake
your head,
June.

I don't realize
I'm doing it.
But still,
I don't stop.

I don't
believe
you.

Again,
I say this
OUT LOUD.

Apparently,
I am now
the sassy
sort of girl
who simply
says what she thinks.

Well,
as sassy
as anyone
can be
while
sobbing.

MY DAD IS DEAD,

Toby announces.

I stare,
shocked.

It takes me
a minute
to realize…

This right here.
THIS is his ugly secret.

I'm sorry,

I say,
unsure now.
Because sure,
it's sad.
But it's not really
an ugly secret.

As if reading
my mind,
Toby adds,

There's more.

*He died of
a drug overdose.*

Big surprise,
        but not really.
He was always a mess.

Mom, too.

Which is why
        I'm staying
                with my grandma.

Mom overdosed
        just like Dad,
only she didn't
        die.

Lucky her.
Ambulance
        got there
                in time.
Stuck some
        magic needle
                in her.
Brought her
        back
                from the dead.

Off she went
                to rehab.

Off I went
                to Grandma's.

Toby stops.
Shrugs.

I'm sorry,

I say again.
It's not enough.

That sucks,

I add.
As if it helps.

Toby shrugs again.

Yeah, well,
        it is what it is.

But do you
       get it now?

  Do you see
    why
      I need things
        at school
     to just be
  easy?

Smooth.
No bumps.
No hassles.

No one
      and
nobody
who will make things
hard.

WHAT CAN YOU SAY

when someone
plays the
dead dad card?

When they
follow it
with the
almost-dead mom card?

I can't say,

Yeah, but Homecoming.

I can't.

And I don't.

We walk
the rest
of the way
home
in silence.

Right before
we part,
Toby asks,

Friends?

I hesitate…
but only
a moment
before answering—

Of course.

Of course,
says the girl
who will not
make his life
hard.

Of course,
says the girl
who holds
his secrets
and nothing
else.

Of course.

THE FRIDAY

of Homecoming
Lacey announces
that Toby's
bringing a date.

She sounds
heartbroken.

And I am
instantly
sick.

I might've
thrown up
if my
stomach
was not
totally
and completely
empty.

I haven't eaten
    a
        single
                bite
in two days.

For once
my lie
is true.

I'm not hungry.

The Friday
of Homecoming
Mae and Erick
have a fight.

He hates
the shortbread cookies.

He calls them
dog biscuits.

He throws them
in her face.

And Mae cries.

I'm sorry,

she tells him.
Sorry.

Sorry for
staying up
all night
making the
shortbread cookies.

Sorry for spending
a week
perfecting
the recipe.

Sorry.

*I got people
wanting to buy
brownies,*

Erick says.

*Nobody wants
    this shortbread
                stuff.
Nobody even knows
            what
                it is.*

Mae again
says she's sorry.

But it's not
good enough.
Not for Erick.

He storms out.
Drives away.

And Mae cries
some more.

The Friday
of Homecoming
I listen to
Mae
crying
in the
bathroom.

I stare
at the
shortbread
sitting on
the kitchen
counter.

I take
the first
bite
to prove
Erick
wrong.

Sweet
butter
and
dark chocolate
chunks
mixed with
little bits
of salt
burst
and
melt
across
my tongue.

That first
bite
I savor.

It's a
miracle
in my
mouth.

I inhale
the rest.

Jaw
working
angrily.

I don't taste
the butter
or chocolate
or salt
as I push
cookie
after
cookie
down
  my
    throat.

I am still
chewing
the last one
when the
sickness
comes.

I run to
the sink,
hang my
head
and…

EXHALE.

Everything
      rushes
           back
               UP.

I'm standing there
panting
when I hear

                  a laugh.

Dude,
that was
sick.

It's Erick.

Erick with
his phone
in hand
recording
everything.

I stare at him.
Mind racing.

And mad.

Not at Erick.
But at me.
For letting
My guard
      D
        O
          W
            N
For not learning
      my lesson.
For letting
    someone lOOk and see.
                Again.

I
didn't
feel
good.

It's the truth.
Sorta.

Erick snickers.

Yeah.
I can tell.

I start to shake.

Please
delete
whatever
you
recorded.

Erick
looks at
his phone.
Like he's
surprised
to see it
in his hand.

Aw, yeah,
*   of course.*
Just goofing
*   with ya.*

He laughs.
Shoves
the phone
in his pocket.

I don't
believe him.
But I have
no power
here.

I try to
take
control.

Or at least
not totally
lose it.

Do you
need something?

110

*I thought
you'd left?*

Erick shrugs.

*Yeah, I
    wanted to
        tell Mae,
she needs
    to make me
        some brownies.
For tonight.
No brownies.
No dancie.*

I know
Erick
is not
the worst
person
on the planet.

I know
there are
murderers
and
child molesters
and even worse
than that still.

But
right now
Erick is
THE WORST.

111

And I am, too.
Because,
I say,

Yeah, okay,
I'll tell Mae.

Erick nods.

Heh, I
figured
you would.

His hand
slaps
my back.
Hard.

You sorta
owe me now,
right?

He looks
at me
and smiles
in a way
that tells me
he won't
be deleting
that video.

I swallow.
And say
nothing.

Erick
squeezes
my shoulder.
Too tight.

Guess
somebody
liked them
ugly cookies.

He's still
laughing
as he
walks out
the door.

MAE ENTERS

the kitchen
not long
after
Erick
leaves.

What's wrong?
She asks
right away.

Erick was
        here.
He wants
        brownies.
Says he
        won't go to
                the dance
        otherwise.

The words are
uneven and stiff.

Mae frowns.
Like she
knows
there's more
I'm not
saying.

Her gaze
lands on
the empty
counter
where her
cookies
used to be.

And he
took the
cookies,
too? she asks.

No,
he
didn't
take
them.

That's all
          I say.

I expect
Mae to ask
where
they went.

She doesn't.
She just
goes silent
and sad.

Even more sad
  than
    before.

And I
  realize.

She knows.

Mae knows
my awful
secret.
Mae has
probably
always known.

And even
though
she knows,
Mae
comes over
and wraps
        her arms
around me.

It'll be okay,

she says.
This is
Mae's
favorite
lie.

Like most
lies,
it's the
thing
we most wish
was true.

WE PRETEND

everything
is fine.

We pretend
everything
is normal.

And we
get ready
for the dance
            together.

I pull
on my dress.
It hangs
on me.

I stare
in dismay
and then
start to
cry.

I brushed
my teeth
and gargled
mouthwash
but I can
still taste
Mae's cookies

coming up
         the wrong way.

Mae comes in,
sees me crying
and then
leaves again.

Moments later
she returns
with her
sewing kit.

C'mon,

she says.

Let's fix you up.

MAE DOES MY HAIR AND MAKEUP

We stand
side by side
looking
in the
mirror.

Our mouths
are two
perfect bows.

Our cheeks
are shaded with
makeup to create
hollows.

Our eyes
are outlined
in black
with eyelashes
sharp and spiky.

I look like Mae.
I look beautiful.

And sad.

In the mirror
my eyes meet
Mae's.

I ask the Mae
in the mirror
what I cannot
ask the Mae
beside me.

Why put up
with him?

Why let him
act that way?
Why not
tell him
to make
his own
brownies?

The Mae
in the mirror
blinks.

Tears shimmer
in her eyes.

I'm sorry,

I say.

And I am.

Mae shakes
her head.

It's okay.
*   I know*
*   he's not…*

Mae stops.
Shakes her head.

Sometimes I think…
*   he's not*
*   worth it.*

Then the Mae
in the mirror
laughs.
Sadly.

But mostly
*   I think*
*   it's okay.*
That being
*   with him,*
being able
*   to say*
"my boyfriend,"
*   is worth it.*

It's the most
honest
Mae has
ever been
with me
about Erick.

Usually she
just says
she loves him.

Maybe only
the Mae
in the mirror
can tell the truth.

What about you? Mae
in the mirror
asks.

She doesn't
ask me.
She asks June
in the mirror.

A girl who
looks like me
mixed with Mae.

Except skinnier.

So skinny
her dress
had to be
taken in
2 inches
on each side.

I'm afraid
you're going to
disappear,

Mae says.

June, when was
the last time
you ate?

Ate and
held it all
in?

Normally,
        I'd lie.

But June
in the mirror
doesn't lie
to Mae
in the mirror.

So, I try
to remember.

Not at lunch.
Not at breakfast.
Not yesterday
for dinner
or lunch
or breakfast
or in between.

The day before?

I remember staring
            at a piece of toast.

Dry.
No butter.
No jelly.

I wanted to eat it.
I needed to eat it.

My hands were
            shaking,
I couldn't hold
            a pen
      to do
         my homework.

I brought
the toast
to my lips.

Took a bite.

It filled
my mouth
expanding
like something
            alive.

I spit it out.
Into a napkin.

That's really
   the
        last time
            I ate.

But that's not
what Mae
in the mirror
means.

When did
I last
EAT,
like really
EAT?

I don't know,

I tell Mae.

Not for
a long,
    long,
      long time.

Mae
in the mirror
frowns.

You know
  that's not
    good...
        don't you?

I look down.

Down at
my feet
without
any shoes.

*I gotta
    finish
        getting ready,*

I say
to Mae
or to Mae
in the mirror
or to no one
at all.

The doorbell
rings.
Lacey's here
to pick
me up.

And then
Erick honks
for Mae
and
we both rush
around,
grabbing
shoes
and purses.

There's no more
Mae or June
in the mirror.

There's no more
truths
to be told.

THIS IS HOW

to attend
a dance
and yet
not be
there
at all.

You sit
at a table
by the
front door
next to
your best friend.

You are
dressed up
like you
are going
to a dance.

But you
do not dance.

Instead
you sit.

Your classmates
come in
and look
through you.

Tickets please,

you say.

They are
laughing
and talking
and having fun.

They do not
hear or
notice
you.

Tickets please,

you repeat.

Someone hears
at last.

They toss
tickets
in your
general direction.

One of the
ticket throwers
is Toby.

For a
moment
his eyes
accidentally
meet yours.

You know
it's an
accident
because
he's smiling,
laughing
at something
the girl
hanging on
his arm
just said.

His gaze
drifts your
way,
finds you,
and
the smile
                    dies.

He almost
seems angry
to see you
there.

Like you
don't belong.

Like you
being there
has ruined
his good
time.

And then
he's gone.

And even
though
it was awful
and he
was awful
you stare
after him
and wish
for so many
things
that cannot
be.

MAE AND ERICK

arrive late.

Her eyes
are glassy,
but her smile
is extra bright
and wide.

We wanted
to make
a dramatic
entrance!

she laughs.

Erick meanwhile
stands
holding a
pretty little plate
stacked
full of frosted
brownies,
looking
     awkward
         and
            angry.

Mae doesn't
usually
frost her brownies.

Too messy,
she says.

She also
doesn't go
much for
presentation.

Normally the
brownies
are packed
in a plastic
container
with a lid.

Easy to
shove into
a backpack
or locker.

It occurs
to me
that Mae
    is messing
        with Erick.

And I like it.

Erick's eyes
lock onto
me
as I take
his ticket.

And this
I do not like.

I can see
some thought
forming
in his
lizard brain.

He smiles.

Mind if I
    leave these
        here?

He asks,
placing the
brownies
in front
of me.

I can
    trust you?
Right, June?
    Not to
        stuff your
           face full
               of them?

Mae swats
at his arm.

Stop that.

But Erick's grin
just grows
W I D E R.

He swivels
his head
to Mae
then back
to me.

*You look
less fat,*

he says to me.

*I noticed
   a bit ago
      and thought
   you must
      be dieting
         or something.*

*Are you dieting,
            June?*

I stare at him
unsure of what
to say.
I'm certain
he means to
out me
no matter
what words
I find.

But Erick
is already
back to Mae,
a slick smile
curling his lips.

How come
    YOU
        can't diet
    like HER?

He says
    to Mae.

Your sister
        knows
    how to
        lose weight.
    Maybe she
            oughtta
        share
    some of her
secrets.

Mae's smile
    finally
        F
        A
            L
            L
            S.

What is
  wrong
    with you?

she hisses.

In response,
Erick's smile
gets wider,
like seeing
Mae unhappy
has been
his goal
this entire
time.

What babe? I'm trying
  to help you
here.
            You know,
      I like a girl
      with something
to grab—

Shockingly,
Erick
actually
shoves
a hand
D
  O
    W
      N

the front of
Mae's dress.

She pushes
him away.

Aw, come on,
       baby.
    Don't be like
        that.

I was
   showing
      everyone—

And to my
horror,
I realize
a crowd
has gathered.

SOMEONE SPOTTED SOMETHING

going on
out here,
away from the
flashing lights
and loud music.

Then word spread.

And now
half the dance
is crowded
into the
entryway
watching.

And Erick loves it.

I was just
showing
everyone,
how much
I love those
c
  u
    r
     v
    e
  s
of yours.

But I
sometimes
wish
there was a
little less
FAT
around them.

He guffaws
at his own
joke.

Some others
join in.
Beside me,
Lacey gasps.

In the crowd
I see several
heads shaking.

I do not
look
at Mae.

I cannot
look
at Mae.

I search the
crowd again,
hoping a
teacher
will come.

A teacher to tell
everyone
to go away.

To tell Erick
he's expelled.

Not just
from school
but from the
entire
human race.

And then I see
                    Toby.

He watches
the scene
seemingly
alone.

Our eyes catch
        and   then   hold.

I wait for him
to step forward.

To tell Erick
to stop.

Because
someone
has to
and Toby can.

Except he doesn't.
Of course
        he doesn't.

Toby has secrets.
Toby does not
want to be seen.

And suddenly
            I hate him.

This friend of mine.
So focused on
        protecting himself.

On worrying
over what
he has to lose.

That he stands there
and lets this happen.

…
…
…

Just like I'm
sitting here.

Letting this happen.

Unable to even look
at Mae.

It hits me.

H A R D.

I'm worse than Toby.

I LOOK AT MAE

The most
beautiful person
I know.

Who sewed
my dress
and did
my makeup
and made
brownies
and still
looks
amazing.

Who now
has her
hands
clasped
over her
chest,
where Erick
reached down
her dress.

She doesn't
seem to notice
Erick
or the crowds
or even me.

Her gaze
is turned
inward
but also
distant.

Like she's
seeing
something
far off
that only
exists
for her.

I look at Mae
and she looks
                    br
              o
                 ke
                    n.

SOMETHING FLARES

inside me.

I shoot
to my
feet.

Look
in
a
mirror!

The words
shout from
my mouth.

You
have
no
neck.

You
have
a face
like
a
stupid,
ugly
caveman!

Lacey gasps.
Mae stares.

The crowd…
            LAUGHS.

You tell him!

some faceless
person yells.

Erick's awful
unibrow
lowers,
making him
look
even more
dumb
and
mean
than usual.

And still
my mouth
WILL
        NOT
                STOP.

Seriously,
you should
see yourself
right now.

Erick stares
a moment
longer.

Then his
mouth purses
as if
getting ready
to spit.

And I know
whatever
comes out
next is
gonna be
awful.

*Dumb loser
and still fat.*

He starts with this.
Which seems
pretty mild.
As bearable
as getting
fat-shamed
in front of
half the school
can be.

But then it
gets worse.

FAT
        because you're
        too dumb
     to eat
less.

Still fat
        because you
        ate all your
sister's cookies.

Still fat
        even though
        you puke up
what you eat.

This
Erick
spits
into
my
face.

So close
I can't look
away.

But now
he turns
to the
crowd.

LOOK,

he says,
fumbling
with his
phone.

LOOK.

He holds
it up,
screen out
so everyone
can see.

I COVER MY FACE

like a
coward.

But I
can still
hear
the
awful
choking,
gagging
sounds
I made
while
barfing up
Mae's
beautiful
shortbread
cookies.

And I am
            not just
embarrassed,
            I am
ashamed, too.

Ashamed
of losing
control.

Ashamed
of my own
uncontrollable
hunger.

The video
goes on
longer than
seems possible.

And then
when it
finally
ends,
Erick asks,

*Who wants to
watch it again?*

Ew, no,

someone says.

And then
a male voice
cuts in.

Dude,
        that's enough.

I uncover
my eyes.

Once again
    hoping to see
                    Toby.

But,
of course,
it's someone else.

A football player
who makes
Erick look small
beside him.

In the
high school sports
pecking order,
football is king.

Erick quickly
lets his phone
fall to his
side.

It's just a joke,

he says.

The football player
shakes his head.

*I think you
owe Mae
and…*

He looks at me,
not knowing
who I am.

That's my sister,
June,

Mae says.

I'd forgotten
Mae was here.

Or maybe I
just couldn't deal
with her shame
and mine
all mixed up
and uncovered
at once.

Except, Mae
doesn't seem
ashamed.

Or sad.

Her chin is
held high
and her
expression
is one
I've never
seen before.

Mae looks
fierce.

She takes
two steps
toward Erick
and plucks
the phone
from his hand.

Hey!

He protests,
but Mae
flicks a
scornful
glance
at him
before
focusing
back on
the phone.

Delete.

She says
the word
aloud.

The awful
   video
   is gone.

No one
can ever
watch it
again.

Tears fill
my eyes.

HEY!

You had no right!

Erick bellows this
as Mae
tosses his
phone back
at him.

She spins
on her heels,
chest heaving.

*YOU had
no right
to come
sneaking
into my
house,
uninvited.*

*YOU had
no right
to blast
June's business
to the whole
school.*

*YOU had
no right
to ruin
this entire
night!*

But you did.
And now
I want you
to leave.

Mae breathes
   heavily.

A few people
   clap.

You tell him,

someone yells.

And more people
 SHOUT
 in agreement.

I REALIZE

with a sudden
shock of surprise:

the crowd
is on Mae's
plus-size side.

I should've
understood
when the
football player
came forward.

But I'd thought
everyone
did the same
math as Mae.

Erick wears
a varsity
jacket.

Mae wears
clothing sizes
not found
in most stores.

She's
lucky
to have him.

That's what
everyone
thinks.

Except they don't.

They see Mae.

Beautiful,
generous
Mae.

They see Erick.

Nasty,
ugly
Erick.

They see them both.

And they picked
           the ~~fat~~
            beautiful girl.

They picked Mae.

ERICK'S LIP CURLS

I'm not leaving.

Mae quickly counters.

Oh yes, you are.
        And take
                your brownies, too.

She picks up
the plate,
balancing it
on one hand,
so everyone
sees it
coming—
except Erick
—who probably
can't believe
she'd do it.

But Mae does it.

She plants that
plate of
brownies
in his mean
face.

THE CROWD GOES WILD

Cheering Mae
loudly,
leaving no
doubts how
they feel.

Erick grabs
Mae's arm,
his fingers
digging into
the soft flesh.

I stand,
pushing
my chair
back with
a screech.

Let her go,

I say,
at the
same time
an adult
finally comes
forward.

That's enough.

His voice
has that ring
of authority.

The crowd parts
and Mr. Mann
instantly
takes control.

Everybody,
back into
the dance
or I'll tell
the DJ to cut
the music
and turn the
lights back on.

There's a groan,
but everyone
knows the best
action has
already passed.

All at once
our audience
is gone.

Mr. Mann
examines
those of us
that remain.

Me,
still standing.

Erick,
still holding
Mae's arm
too tight.

Mae,
licking
chocolate
frosting
from her fingers
without a hint
of regret.

And Lacey.
Still sitting
at the table,
stunned
          and silent.

IT'S ALWAYS SOMETHING,

Mr. Mann says,
and there's a
hint of laughter
in his voice.

Suddenly,
I am very glad
Mr. Mann
is here tonight.

He is known
as the guidance counselor
you can tell
almost
the whole truth to.

When I
first saw
him coming
I felt sick
knowing
come Monday
a note will
arrive
asking me to
visit him
                    ASAP.

Because he will
have heard about the video.

And he will
want to talk
          about it.

As much as
I dread that,
another
part of me
knows…
          it's for the best.

Another part
          of me
thinks
I'll tell Mr. Mann
most
of the truth.

Another part
          of me
thinks I should've
talked to Mr. Mann
a long time ago.

TIME TO GO

Mr. Mann
tells Erick,
a hand
on his elbow,
already
guiding him
toward the door.

Wait!
What about Mae?

Erick points.

She, she, she
ASSAULTED
me.

Mr. Mann
laughs.

Assault? With...
      brownies?

She did,

Erick keeps at it.

Where are you hurt?

Mr. Mann asks,
and now Erick
is almost out
the door.

Erick hesitates.
The door is
closing behind
him, as he
finally answers,

She got some
frosting
in my eye.

It really HURTS!

The door closes.

Erick is gone.

MY LEGS TURN TO RUBBER

I sink into
my chair.

Lacey unfreezes
        at last.
She hops to
        her feet.

*I'll just give
        you two
                a...*

And then
she's gone,
disappeared
into the dance.

I wonder
if she'll
ever talk to me
again.

Suddenly,
    Mae's arms
        wrap around
    me.

I hug her
right back.

We hold
one another
a long time.

Not crying,
just breathing
and surviving
            together.

I'm sorry,

I whisper at last.

Mae pulls back
a few inches,
her hands
still connecting us.

*You got nothing
to be sorry for,*

she says,
looking like
fierce Mae again.

But Erick…

I start to say,
        but Mae
        shakes her head.

Erick was awful.

Maybe not
  at the beginning,
      but most of the time.
And I just let him
              be awful.
To me.
And to you,
          June.

I'm the one
    who should
        be saying sorry.

Now it's
my turn
to shake
my head.

No, don't.

Mae nods
and we hug
again.

NOW WHAT?

I ask,
at last.

Mae stands.

Now we dance.

She holds a hand
out to me.

I stare at it.
Then look at
the flashing lights
in the gym
and all the bodies
moving through it.

Bodies belonging
to people
who saw that video.

Sure they were
on Mae's side,
but most of them
barely know me.

I'll be known
forever
as the
puking girl.

*Better to get it
over with,*

Mae says softly,
reading my mind.

She's right.
I know this.

But I'm not ready.

*Give me a minute,
            please?*

Mae frowns.
Then nods.

A minute,

she says,
  sternly.
    And then
  she goes
      into the gym,
  disappearing
      into the mass
  of bodies.

I SIT ALONE

trying to
process
everything
that went
down.

Trying to
decide
where I
fit
and what
I should
do next.

Eat,
I realize.
I should
eat.

Or try to
eat.

Like a
normal
person
who doesn't
count bites
and calories.

And, I should…

My thoughts stall
as Toby
comes out
of the gym
to stand
before me.

I stare.

Are you okay? he asks,
hands stuffed
in his pants pockets.

I shrug.

Right.

He nods.

Well,
I'm heading out.
  I thought
    you might
      wanna walk home
                  with me.

I can imagine it.
Just like the
      other night.

Toby and me
    together
    in the dark,
        holding hands,
    spying on
        anyone with open
    curtains,
        owning secrets
    that aren't
    ours to have.

What about
        your date? I ask.

Oh. Her,

Toby says.

He grins
    with half
    his mouth.

She wasn't
    really my date.
I was doing
    a favor
        for a friend.
He's been hooking
    up with her,
        but his girlfriend
            doesn't know.

So he asked me
        to help him out.

I think they snuck
            away
                    together
        a while ago.

Toby laughs.
Like any of this
is funny.

That's awful,
I say.

What about
his girlfriend?

Toby shrugs.

Well, my friend
    thinks she cheated
            on him first,
                    so...

Another shrug.

Everyone has secrets.

He says this
like it makes
everything okay.

Like one secret
crosses out another.

So whaddya say? Toby holds out
his hand.

*Wanna get out
of here?*

I STARE AT TOBY'S HAND

Wanting—
    despite everything
        —to take it.

June?

Lacey calls my name.

I see her
standing
in the doorway
of the gym.

I don't know
how long
she's been there.

Suddenly,
Toby drops
his hand.

Shoves it
back in his
pocket.

I'll be outside,

he says to me
softly, so
Lacey won't hear.

And then
        he's gone
out the door.

But not
        really gone.
Because
        he's waiting
for me.

Certain I
        won't say no.

How can he
be so certain
when even I don't know
what I want
to do?

Lacey,
her head tipped
to the side
like a curious
little bird
comes toward me,
cautious
and uncertain.

You okay? she asks.

It's funny
to hear Lacey
ask the same question
as Toby.

I give her the
  same lame
          shrug.

She nods.
Then her
glance flickers
toward the door
Toby
just exited through.

I can see her
dying to ask
what he said,
why he was
even talking
            to me.

*He lives
next door,*

I tell her.

Lacey's mouth
  falls open.

This whole time?

I nod.

I expect her
to be mad.
But it's hurt
that fills
Lacey's face.

But...
why didn't
you tell me?

she asks.

I hesitate,
and then tell
the truth.
Or part of it.

He saw me
puking.

Outside
in the shrubs
in the back
of my house.

I was...
embarrassed.

Lacey gasps,
a hand
covering
her mouth.

Oh no.

Oh, June.
I had no idea.
And all those times
I went on and on
about him.

Lacey shakes her head.

He's not even
that great.
He's borrowed
so many pens
from me.
Like I have
an endless supply
and he never gives
them back!
In fact,
he gave one
of my pens
to someone else
and then asked me
for another!

Like that's all
I am.
The girl with pens
               for everyone!

Lacey stops.
Frowns.

But this is about you.
Sorry, June.

I'm sorry that
                    jerk
knew and I didn't.
I mean,
      I knew you
            didn't eat much.
I thought…
      it was just a diet.
But I should've known.
I should've seen.

Unexpectedly,
      she grabs my hands.

I'm so sorry, June.

Lacey's eyes
glisten with tears.
And I can see
she means it.

Suddenly,
I can't remember
why I've been
shutting her out
all this time.

Suddenly,
it seems like
I almost lost
my best friend.

*Is there
anything
I can do?* Lacey asks.
Then she
laughs.

*I mean, besides
    not eating your
        lunches for you
    anymore?*

And surprisingly,
                I laugh, too.

It's okay,

I say.

*I was just gonna
throw it out
anyway.*

But Lacey
shakes her head.

*But not anymore.
                June…
You gotta stop this.
I had a cousin with…*

Again Lacey hesitates.

I can hear her
holding back
an uglier word.

Instead she says,

My cousin had
        eating problems
                and ended up
        in the hospital
                because of them.

She had to
        drop out of college.
By then, it'd been
        going on for years.
And nobody knew.

June—

She squeezes my hands.

We can't let that happen to you.

I squeeze back.

I know,
I say softly,
the shame
still there,
keeping my voice low.

I know.

I'm gonna work on it
        and get help or
                whatever I need.
I know
      it's gotta stop.

Lacey smiles
      big and wide.
And then
      shakes herself.

I forgot! Mae sent me out! She can't get away!
Everyone wants
to dance with her
or give her high fives.
There's a rumor
already going around
that she put—

Lacey lowers
her voice
to a whisper.

—some poop
in the brownies
she splatted
Erick with.

Lacey laughs.
And I can't help
but join in.

She would never do that! I protest.

Lacey waves this away.

Oh, I know.
But it's so funny.
Mae is like a…
                    hero.

I am stunned silent
    as a bubble of
        happiness grows
                in my chest.

Anyway,

Lacey flaps
her hands
bringing my
attention
back to her.

Mae says
to get your butt
inside.
Now.
It's time to dance.

Lacey stands.
Holds a hand out.

The same way
Toby did.
Toby…
     still waiting outside
for me.

I can see
two roads
splitting,
depending
on which
          hand
I take.

A quiet, dark
street with Toby.
His hand in mine,
a secret,
just like the ones
in every house
along the road.

Everyone has secrets.

But I don't.
Not anymore.
The whole school
saw mine.

And I survived.
I will survive.
Maybe do more
than survive.
Maybe it'll even
make me better.

I think,
for now,
I've had
enough
secrets.

I think
it's time to take
the second road,
the one with
flashing lights
and pounding music.

The one with
Mae dancing,
not worrying
about how
she jiggles.

The one with
Lacey,
a friend,
holding out her hand,
and offering
to help.

I TAKE LACEY'S HAND

and I dance
all night.

Sometimes,
I think about
that dark road
and Toby walking
alone along it.

But then
Mae's hip
    BUMPS
      against mine
and I
    BUMP
      her back.

A song comes on
about powerful women
loving themselves.

We sing along.

As loud as we can.

WANT TO KEEP READING?

If you liked this book, check out another book
from West 44 Books:

WATCHES AND WARNINGS
BY RYAN WOLF

ISBN: 9781538382714

THE CELLAR

"It's always wise
to worry
about the wind.
When it gets
tired of our
little farms and schools
and grocery stores,
it will kick
them down.
It'll shake us
into the
sky."

Mr. Gregor likes
to talk this way
as we replace
old soup cans
with new ones
on his steel shelves.

We sweep
the concrete floors.
Check the dates
on medicines
in his first aid kits.
Drill together
new racks.
Fill them
with supplies.

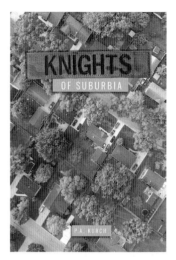

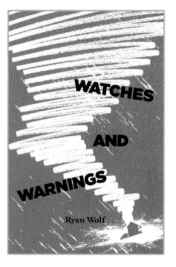

Check out more books at:
www.west44books.com

An imprint of Enslow Publishing

WEST **44** BOOKS™

ABOUT THE AUTHOR

Kate Karyus Quinn is an avid reader and menthol chapstick addict. After living in both California and Tennessee, she returned to her hometown of Buffalo, New York, and now lives there with her husband, three children, and one enormous dog. She is the author of young adult novels *Another Little Piece, (Don't You) Forget About Me,* and *Down with the Shine.*